Disney · PIXAR

MONSTERS
UNIVERSITY

ROARING RIVALS

ADAPTED BY TENNANT REDBANK
ILLUSTRATED BY GEEFWEE BOEDOE

A Random House PICTUREBACK® Book
Random House 🏠 New York

ISBN: 978-0-7364-3041-8

randomhouse.com/kids

Printed in the United States of America

10 9 8 7 6 5 4 3 2 1

P9-DNT-816

Mike and Sulley were monsters who were nothing alike. Mike was short and round. Sulley was big and furry. Mike worked hard. Sulley liked to have a good time.

But the two monsters had one thing in common. They'd come to Monsters University to go to the School of Scaring. They wanted to learn how to be really scary monsters!

One night, Mike was in his room studying when the rival school's mascot popped through his window! Sulley came in right behind it. Sulley had stolen the mascot to impress the Roar Omega Roars, the coolest, scariest monsters on campus.

Sulley and Mike chased the mascot all over campus. Mike caught it—but Sulley got the credit! The RORs invited Sulley to join their group, but not Mike.

"You're just not in the same league with me," Sulley told Mike.

"I'm gonna scare circles around you this year," Mike replied.

After that, Mike studied twice as hard. He knew the textbooks by heart. He practiced roars and scary faces. He just *had* to beat the fur off Sulley on the final exam! Meanwhile, Sulley spent his time having fun with the RORs.

On the day of the final, the head of the School of Scaring, Dean Hardscrabble, came to watch. Years before, the dean had broken the all-time scream record. Her legendary scream canister had a place of honor in the classroom.

As they waited for their turns, Mike and Sulley started to show off their scares. Mike roared at Sulley. Sulley roared at Mike. Mike roared louder. Sulley roared louder, then—whoops! Sulley bumped into the dean's scream canister and destroyed it!

Dean Hardscrabble was so angry she kicked Mike and Sulley out of class! Mike was heartbroken. He had wanted to be a Scarer ever since he was a little monster. Sulley was unhappy, too—the only thing he was good at was being scary.

Then Mike had an idea. He would enter the Monsters University Scare Games to prove just how scary he was! But none of the teams wanted Mike—except the Oozma Kappas. Mike made a bet with the dean. If his team won, she'd let them into the School of Scaring.

SCARE
GAMES

There was one catch. Each team needed six monsters. Mike's
team only had five. Suddenly, Sulley volunteered.

"No way!" Mike shouted. But he had no choice. He needed
Sulley on his team. And secretly, Sulley thought the Oozma
Kappas were the least frightening monsters he'd ever seen.

The first event of the Scare Games was a race through a tunnel filled with stinging glow urchins. Whichever team came in last would be out of the games.

Mike and Sulley tied in second place—but the rest of the Oozma Kappas came in last. Then one of the other teams got kicked out for cheating, which meant the Oozma Kappas would go on to the next round!

After the first challenge, Mike realized he couldn't win on his own. He had to bring the team together. But no one else believed the Oozma Kappas could ever be scary enough to win. Not Dean Hardscrabble. Not the RORs. And especially not Sulley.

"We're going on a little field trip," Mike said. The trip was to Monsters, Inc., the factory where all the best Scarers worked.

Monsters, Inc. didn't have just one kind of Scarer. They came in all shapes and sizes. Every great Scarer was scary in his or her own way.

At last, Sulley—and the Oozma Kappas—understood that a monster didn't need sharp claws and big teeth to be scary.

After their visit to Monsters, Inc., the Oozma Kappas started training hard and working together. They made it through the Scare Games until finally only the RORs and the Oozma Kappas were left!

But Sulley was still worried that Mike wasn't scary enough to win the Scare Games.

The final challenge was the hardest—the Scare Simulator. The RORs and the Oozma Kappas showed off their best scares.

Mike went last. When it was his turn . . . *ROAR!* He filled the scream can right to the top! The Oozma Kappas had won!

Mike was so happy, he gave another tiny "boo!" The can filled back up again! Mike checked the control panel. It was on the easiest level! Sulley had secretly reset the controls.

Sulley quickly realized that he had let Mike—and his team—down by cheating.

Mike wanted to prove once and for all that he was scary. He broke into the school's lab and sneaked through a door into the human world! Mike found a cabin full of kids to scare.

But the kids weren't scared. They thought he was cute!

Sulley was worried. All monsters knew that children were toxic. Sulley went to rescue Mike.

Sulley found his friend and let him know he was sorry. Mike agreed to return with him, but Dean Hardscrabble had turned off the power in the lab. They were stuck in the human world!

There was only one way back. They had to generate enough
scream energy to power the door from the human side.
Working together, they came up with plan for a super scare—
and then they created the biggest scream ever!

Back at Monsters University, the light over the door glowed
with energy as Mike and Sulley burst through!

Mike and Sulley made a great team, but that didn't keep them from getting kicked out of school. They'd broken too many rules.

But they'd also changed Dean Hardscrabble's mind. "I was wrong about you," she told them. She believed in them—just as they had come to believe in each other.

Mike had a new plan—he and Sulley would get jobs at Monsters,
Inc.! They could work their way up to being Scarers.

"Whaddaya say?" he asked Sulley, his new best friend.

Sulley grinned at Mike. "I'm in if you are!"